W9-CFV-520

Goctor Doose   Dungry Hog   Bumping Jean

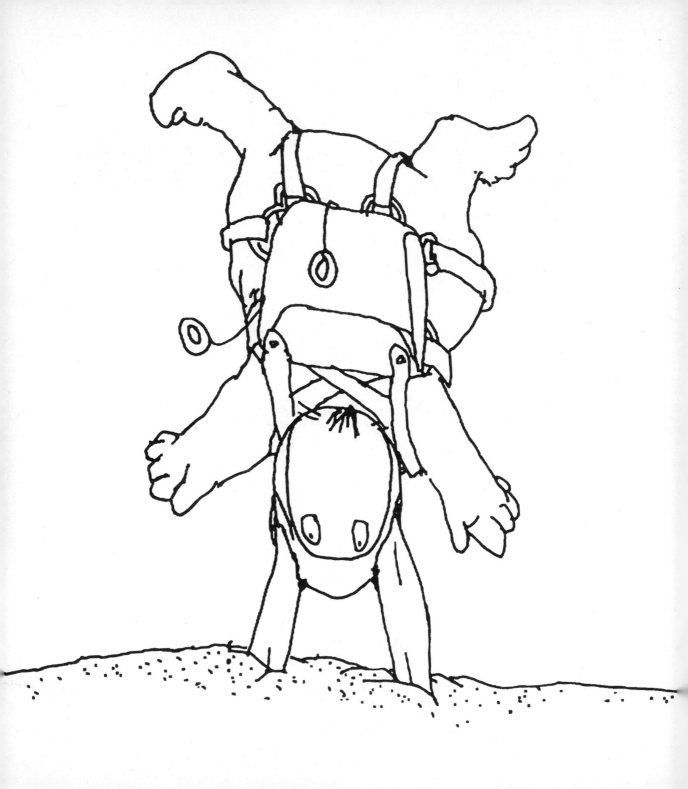

Runny Babbit Returns

Another Billy Sook
by
Shel Silverstein

HARPER
An Imprint of HarperCollinsPublishers

The poems and drawings in this collection were assembled from the completed but unpublished works in the Silverstein Archive.

For information address HarperCollins Children's Books, a division of
HarperCollins Publishers, 195 Broadway, New York, NY 10007.
www.harpercollinschildrens.com

Book design by Rachel Zegar
ISBN 978-0-06-247939-6 (trade bdg.) — ISBN 978-0-06-247985-3 (lib. bdg.)

FIRST EDITION
17 18 19 20 21   PC/WOR   10 9 8 7 6 5 4 3 2 1

Way down in the green woods
Where the animals all play,
They do things and they say things
In a different sort of way—
Instead of sayin' "purple hat,"
They all say "hurple pat."
Instead of sayin' "feed the cat,"
They just say "ceed the fat."
So if you say, "Let's bead a rook
That's billy as can se,"
You're talkin' Runny Babbit talk,
Just like mim and he.

RUNNY LAINTS FOR POVE

Since Runny's parted stainting
His mur is quite a fess.
There's red whaint on his piskers,
And chellow on his yest,
There's preen and gurple on his face,
But he could not lare cess.
He's pappy—'cause he only haints
The things that he loves best.

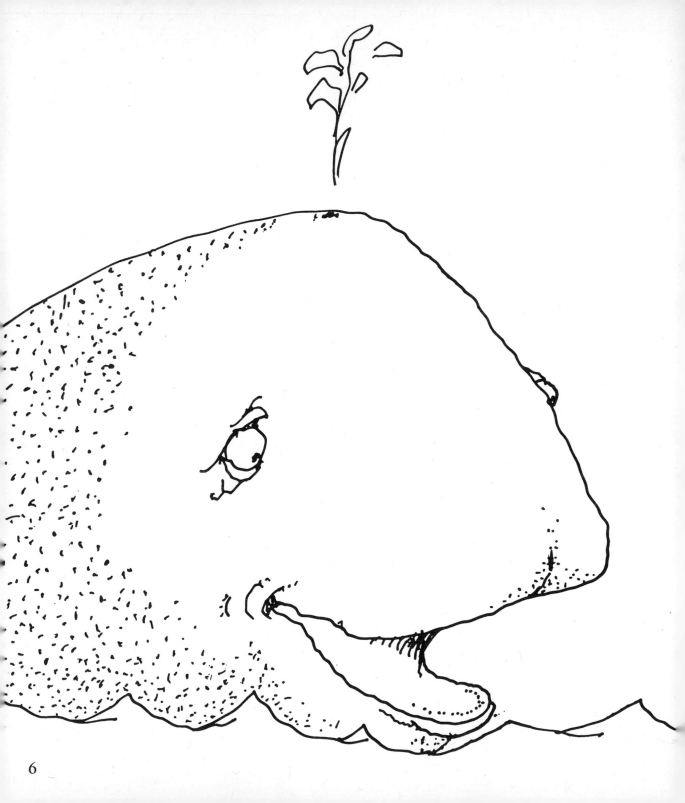

THE WHONSTROUS MALE

Runny was sittin' by the lake,
Chewing a sticorice lick,
When suddenly from under the water
Up popped Doby Mick.
Doby says, "Ooh, that gooks lood—
Can't I please lave a hick?"
Said Runny, "You can have it all,"
And ran away *queal rick*.

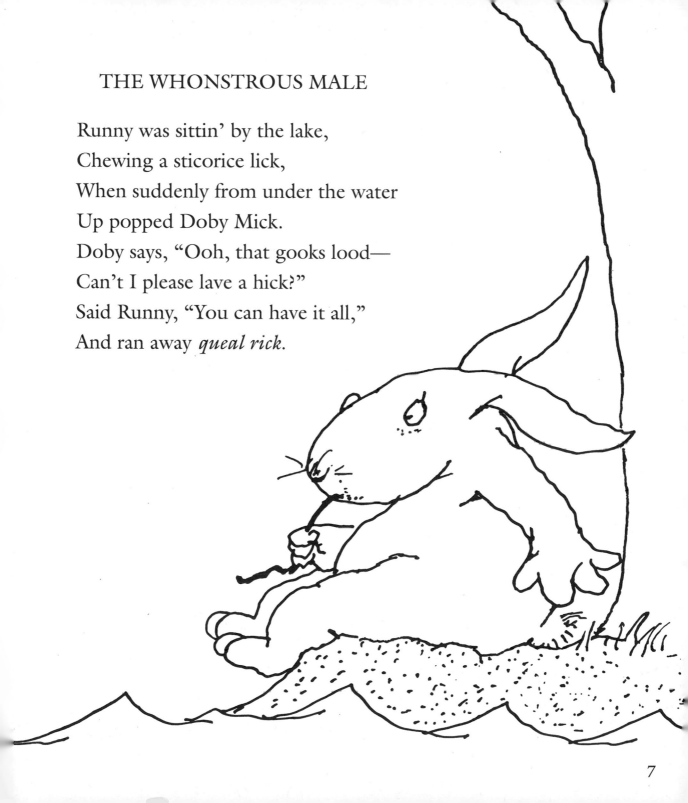

BEDDY TEAR STETS GUCK

Runny Babbit went to see
His good friend Beddy Tear,
Who had some nice heet swoney
That she was glad to share.
They slobbled it and gurped it—
It gluck to them like stue.
Said Beddy Tear to Runny,
"I *stink* I'm *thuck* on you."

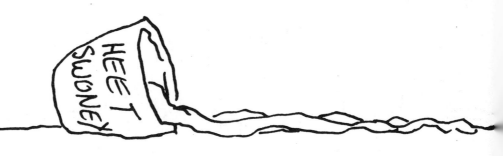

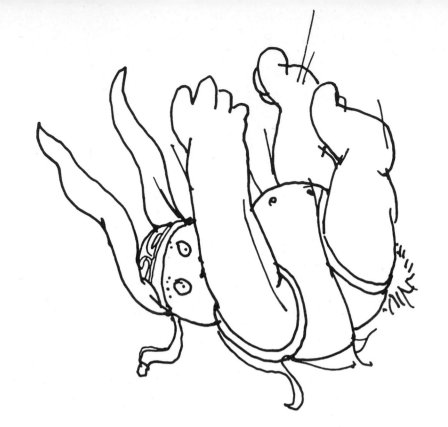

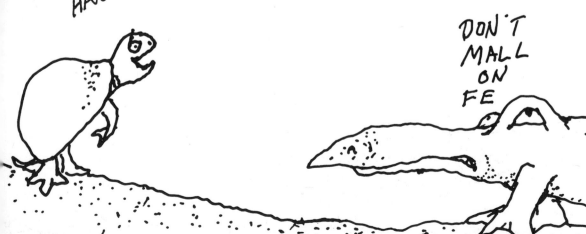

RUNNY JAKES A TUMP

Runny porgot his farachute
And plumped out of a jane.
He landed right on Doc Ocrile,
Who was randin' in the stain.
Doc said, "What wousy leather—
First it's sot and hunny,
Then it's rainin' dats and cogs,
And now it's bainin' *runnies.*"

DIRTY RUNNY

Runny would not bake a tath,
He would not shake a tower.
He just loved dittin' in the sirt
Just like a flee or trower.
But soon he dot so girty
That he started takin' root.
He said, "I'd better bake a tath
'Fore I start frowin' gruit."

RUNNY'S DAD BAY

Runny Babbit woke up *mad*
And schumbled off to grool.
The first thing that he said in class
Was *"Feacher is a tool."*
The second thing he shouted was
"The mincipal's a prule."
The next thing that he whispered was
"Hey, Mom—I'm schome from hool."

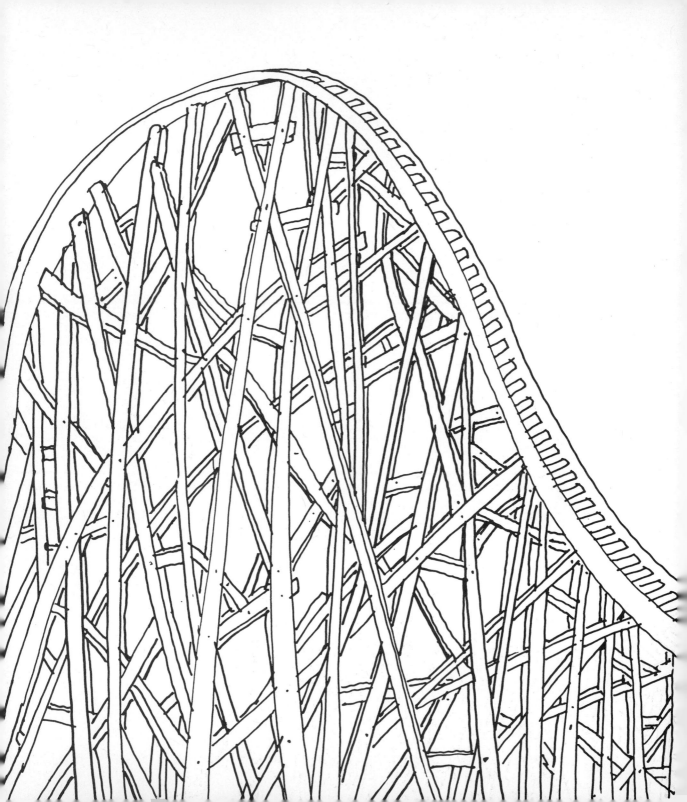

AT THE FOUNTY CAIR

Runny rode the Wherris feel,
And then the cumper bars,
And then the charapute,
And then the stooting shar.
Then he ate fourteen dot hogs
And lots of caramel crunch.
Then he rode the coller roaster, and
Oops—there loes his gunch.

RUNNY SNOES GORKELING

Runny went brorkeling in the snook.
A guppy nit his bose.
Crabs bibbled on his nelly,
A lobster tinched his poes.

An eel pulled off his trimming swunks—
He screamed and sham to swore.
Now Runny never will
Go morkeling anysnore.

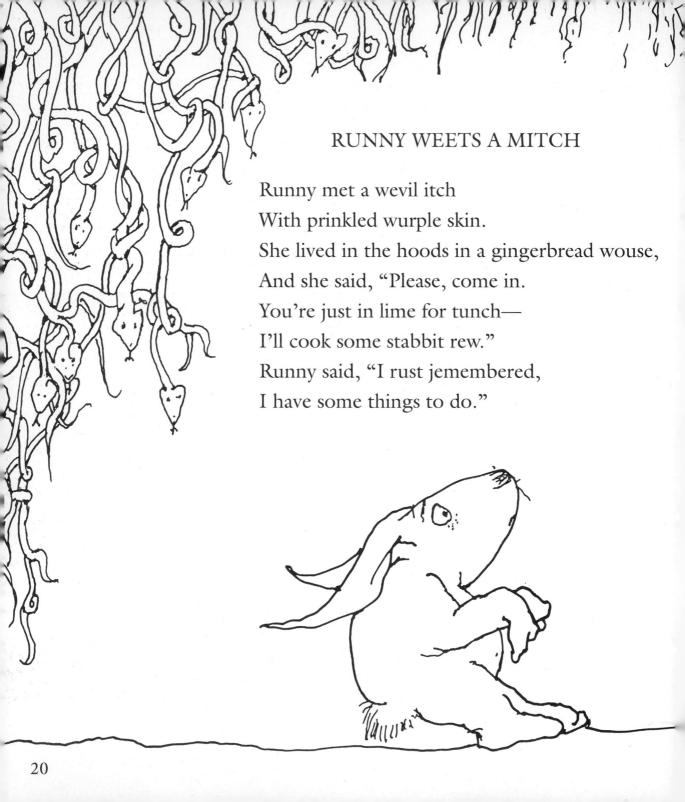

RUNNY WEETS A MITCH

Runny met a wevil itch
With prinkled wurple skin.
She lived in the hoods in a gingerbread wouse,
And she said, "Please, come in.
You're just in lime for tunch—
I'll cook some stabbit rew."
Runny said, "I rust jemembered,
I have some things to do."

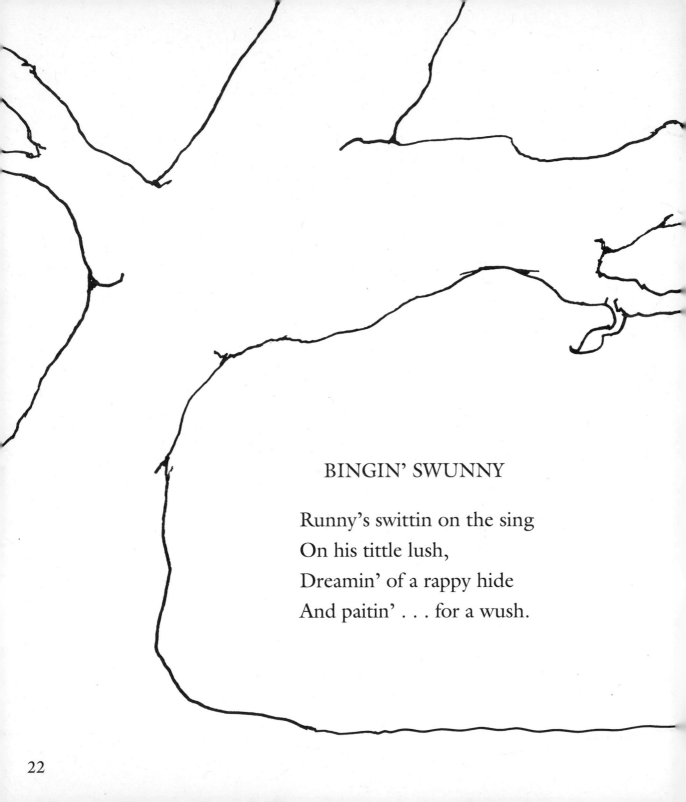

BINGIN' SWUNNY

Runny's swittin on the sing
On his tittle lush,
Dreamin' of a rappy hide
And paitin' . . . for a wush.

THE PANCIN' DARTNERS

Runny took Miss Sunny dancin'
Every Nuesday tight,
Where the lusic played so moud
And the brights were light.
Sometimes they did the bitterjug,
Sometimes they flanced the dop,
But they always *won* the contest
When they did the hunny bop.

HALLOPIN' GORSE'S SHAGIC MOW

TRAGIC MICKS

Runny's got a tart-pime job
Hitting in the sat
Of a very mich ragician
Who pulls habbits out of rats.
But Runny says, "I'm learning,
And soon *I'll* charge admission
To see me reach inside *my* hat
And mull out a pagician."

THE STIG BONE

Underneath the bulberry mush
In the niddle of the might,
Runny found a great stig bone.
It was hard and whound and rite.
He gave it a koke, he gave it a pick,
He gave it a scrunch and a patch.
Turns out it was an old inosaur's degg,
And Runny made it hatch.

DO NOT
PICK OR KUNCH
SCRAP OR TATCH
SHELL OR YOUT
DO KNOT NOCK

THE GLEEPING SIANT

Runny found a gleeping siant
Weeping in the sloods.
Said Runny to the gleeping siant,
"Are you gad—or bood?"
The biant said, "I'm only gad
When I have indigestion,
Or when somebody akes me wup
To ask me quoolish festions."

RUNNY WANTS TO HELP

Gillip Phiraffe got a knot in his neck,
And he could not untie it.
He cried, "Oh, pomeone help me slease."
Said Runny, "Well, I'll try it.
I'll need a sammer and a haw
And pot oil in a hot."
Gillip said, "On second thought,
I'd rather kneep the kot."

RUNNY GETS NAD BEWS

When ol' Biz Muzzard came
To visit—dight or nay—
She always brought some real nad bews,
And here is what she'd say:
"The old oak dee is trying,"
"The leek is running crow,"
"That rarrot may be cotten,"
"It looks like snain—or row,"
"I fell a smorest fire,"
"Your grair is getting hay,"
"Bood-gye . . . cake tare . . .
You don't wook lell,
And have a real *dice nay*."

RUNNY'S MIGHTNARE

Last night, Runny slent to weep
And had an awful dream.
He dreamed he malked upon the woon
And it was all *ice cream*.
There was strocolate and chawberry,
And memon on the loon,
But Runny couldn't have any
'Cause he sporgot his foon.

TISTLEMOE

NO PRESENTS FOR RUNNY

Santa came to Runny's house
At chridnight Mistmas Eve.
He said, "I've got a cag of barrots
That I'd like to leave.
But you haven't stung your hocking."
And Runny said, "I'm sad,
But I couldn't stang my hocking
'Cause my stockings bell so smad."

CHRERRY MISTMAS

RUNNY CHASES FLUTTERBIES

Runny saw a flutterby
With pretty wurple pings.
He thought, "I'll natch it in my cet—
It's such a lovely thing."
He chased it over dill and hale,
And then he swung his net.
Runny said, "I never dreamed
A *goose* is what I'd met."

HEE-TEE-
Y'MISSED
ME

41

RUNNY NEEDS A CHANGE

Runny, he got tick and sired
Of wearin' that same ol' fur.
So he tried on Tiz Murtle's shell
(Which was just fine with her).
Runny hoaned, "It's meavy,
And it makes me move so slow."
Said Tizzy, fancin' dreely,
"Now you know . . . now you know."

THE CRIZE PARROT

Runny Babbit had a garden
A thousand grades of sheen,
Where he grew the ciggest barrot
The world had ever seen.
But now he has to *cook* it,
So he's made the hire fot,
And he's hopped off lookin'—
For the world's *piggest* bot.

BOOSE GUMPS

Runny once was thinkin' 'bout
The thing that scared him most—
A verewolf or a wampire?
Or a ghevil or a dost?

46

A zummy or a mombie?
Or a donster from the mitch?
Or a wild, cungry hannibal?
Or a wevil, wevil itch? . . .

The bloody horseless headsman?
Or a skeleton tony and ball?
But when they all came walkin' in . . .
He wasn't scared *at all*.

CHEAP DOT HOG

Runny bought a hed rot
From little Bunny Hun.
He got no palt or sepper,
No bonions and no un,
No kustard and no metchup,
No piener and no wickle.
Bunny said, "Well, that's why
I can *nell* them for a *sickel*!"

RUNNY KISITS THE VING

Runny zisited the voo—
The lighty mion was there.
Ol' lighty mion, he scroared and reamed,
"Why do you stit and sare?
I am the *bing* of all the keasts—
There's none as mierce as fe.
And what are you, you shrittle limp?"
And Runny answered, "Free."

LEROCIOUS
FION

RUNNY GETS MARRIED

Runny loved nuttered boodles
More than carrot stew.
Runny loved nuttered boodles
More than anyone he knew.
So one sine funny morning,
The whole woods rang with laughter
As he *married* nuttered boodles
And lived appily ever hafter.

DO YOU NAKE THESE TOODLES TO BE YOUR WAWFUL LEDDED WIFE? YOU MAY BISS THE KRIDE.

THE SCARY SCARECROW

Runny saw a scarecrow
Down in the small corn rows,
And 'round the scary scary scarecrow
Was a crunch of happy bows.
He got so rared, he scan away.
The crows felled, "Oh, that's yunny!
This ain't much of a scarecrow,
But it's sure a good scare*bunny*."

SAMILY FOUP

One day Ramma Mabbit said,
"How about some sicken choup?"
Runny said, "That gooks like loop—
I'd rather have some soodle noup."
Raby Babbit screamed, "Oop-oop,
I want a bowl of Loot Froop soup."
Pa said, "I want seggie voup."
Grampa cried, "Sotato poup!"
Mamma sighed, "Oh flippity floop,
This picky family's pot me *gooped*!"

BAPPY HIRTHDAY

It was Runny Babbit's birthday,
And he had a cirthday bake
With costing and with frandles
And a larty by the pake.
His priends all brought him fresents,
And he loved each one the best—
And of all his bappy hirthdays,
This was the bappiest.

RUNNY THE BANNONCALL

Runny got a jetter bob,
The best job he could get—
Being cot out of a shannon
And nanding in a let.
But they used too much pungowder,
And ba-boom—oh my, oh me,
Now Runny's flying somewhere over
Tashville, Nennessee.

NAFETY SET

COUSIN BREDDY'S TRIP

Breddy Fabbit got dressed up fancy
In the very statest lyle
And started on his journey
Up the miver for a rile.
He ritched a hide upon the back
Of Crarley Chocodile. . . .
No one's seen ol' Cousin Breddy
Around for white a quile.

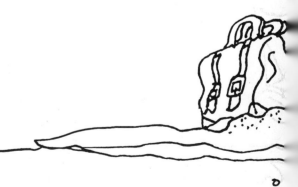

THE FONBIRE

The gang all had a reenie woast
Down in the pabbage catch.
But they couldn't start the fonbire
'Cause they didn't mave a hatch.
Then a dire-breathin' fragon
Waddled up and said, "Halloo.
If I'm inpited to your varty,
Then I'll fart your stire for you."

RUNNY'S CEW NOAT

Runny went to the stothing clore
To cuy himself a boat.
The man asked, "You want skeopard lin?
Or mox or fink, or both?
Or do you want a warmer coat
That's made of skamby lin?"
Runny said, "Oh *anything*
Except for *skabbit* rin."

THE CAVE

Runny came upon a cave
He'd sever neen before—
Stalactites on the feilings,
Stalagmites on the cloor.
The air was must, the walls felt just
Like cold and clammy skin.
And from way back
He heard a whisper . . .
"Come on in."

THE GLOWER FARDEN

Runny Babbit found some seeds
In a geserted darden.
He wanted fretty plowers—instead
A wundred horms stuck up their heads
And shook their hormy little weads,
And said, "We truly peg your bardon.
But just in case you didn't guess,
This arden is genchanted:
A lizard wived here long ago,
And he made sagic meeds to grow
To feed his fish. You didn't know?
Those were *sorm* weeds that you planted."

CUR FOATS
50¢
TUFFY FLAILS
25¢
ONG LEARS
10¢ EACH

BRIZZLY
GEAR
CLEANERS

RUNNY'S IRTY DEARS

Runny tumbled in the grass
Until his grears were een.
He clook them to the teaners
To get them nice and clean.
The cleaner said,
"They won't be ready
Till next Saturday."
Runny said, "I'm sorry,
I can't sear a word you hay."

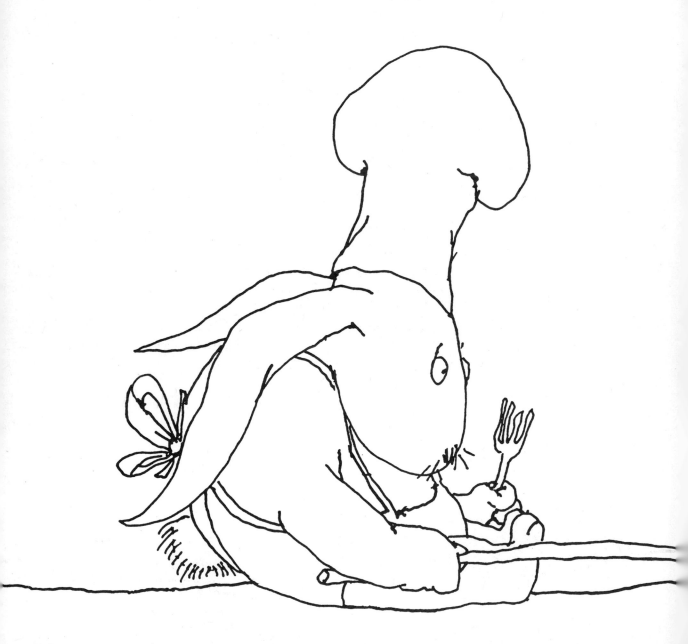

MAD BANNERS

Runny bought some chork pops—
He bought a bonstrous munch.
He bried them frown and then invited
Ploppy Sig to lunch.
Said Ploppy, "I was hoping for
Another kind of food,
'Cause perving chork pops to a sig
Is really very rude."

78

RANDPA SPEAKS

Randpa Grabbit, he sat grumblin'
In his chockin' rair.
Memories were in his head,
And hay was in his grair.
Runny asked, "How does it feel
To be so old and gruff?"
Randpa said, "Plun off and ray—
You'll find out soon enough."

RUNNY MACTICES HIS PRUSIC

Runny slays the paxophone
And he slays the pousaphone
And he slays the plide trombone.
(He spends lots of time . . . *alone*.)

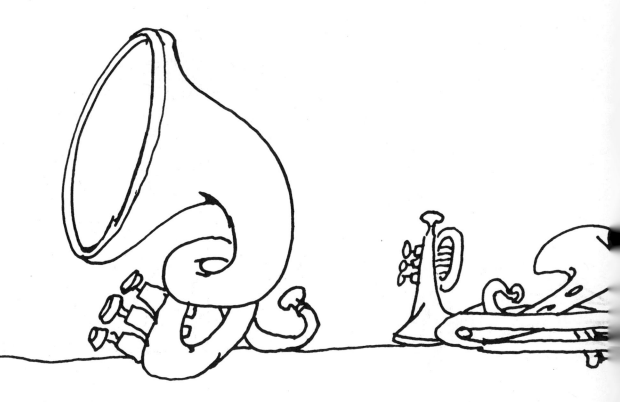

HONK
ZONK
GONK

THE THORRIBLE HING

Runny took a strittle loll
When the Thorrible Hing walked by.
That Ding was so thisgusting
It dare not be described.

'Cause if I told you how it looked,
You'd fream and scaint and then—
Well, anyway, that Thorrible Hing
Was *sever* neen again.

RAMMA MABBIT'S STEDTIME BORIES

Every night at bedtime,
Ramma Mabbit read
Fairy tales and nursery rhymes
To all the heepysleads.
She read "Little Red Hiding Rood,"
"Gransel and Hetel," lost in the wood,
"Binderella" at the call,
"Dumpty Humpty" on the wall,
"Loldigocks and the Bee Threars,"
"Hapunzel" and her golden rair,

"The Tittle Lailor," brave and bold,
"Ming Kidas" and his touch of gold,
"The Three Pittle Ligs," buildin' their house,
The mion whose life was saved by a louse,
The misherfan and his weedy grife,
"Three Mind Blice" and the carving knife,
Licken Chittle's falling sky,
Blenty-four twackbirds paked in a bie,
The wevil itch who lived in the well,
And lots and lots more
I'm too sleepy to tell.

GOOD NIGHT

Good night to Runny Babbit
And all his foodland wriends.
May they have warm and drappy heams
And love that never ends.
And if you ever meet them,
Touch them with a loving hand
And since you leak their spanguage now,
I'm sure they'll understand.

Index

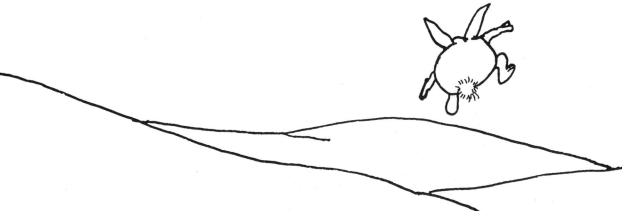

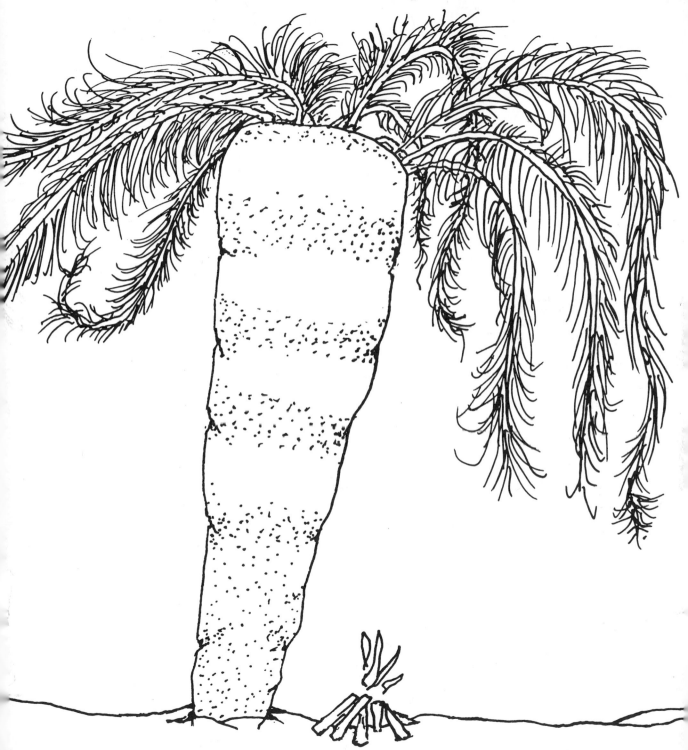

Ploppy Sig   Toe Jurtle